ATTACK OF THE DINOBOTS!

Library of Congress catalog card number: 2007933980
ISBN 978-0-06-088806-0
09 10 11 12 13 LP/UG 10 9 8 7 6
❖
First Edition

ATTACK OF THE DINOBOTS!

ADAPTED BY AARON ROSENBERG

BASED ON THE EPISODE "BLAST FROM THE PAST" WRITTEN BY KEVIN HOPPS

HarperEntertainment

An Imprint of HarperCollinsPublishers

Optimus Prime, Ratchet, Prowl, Bulkhead, and Bumblebee decide to visit Dino-World. The Autobots want to learn about the history of their new home, Earth.

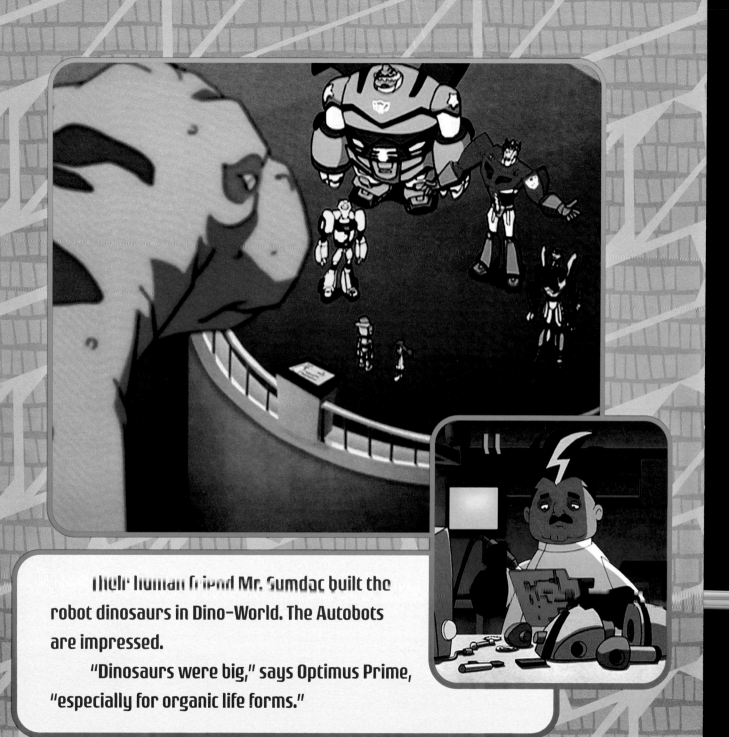

Their human friend Mr. Sumdac built the robot dinosaurs in Dino-World. The Autobots are impressed.

"Dinosaurs were big," says Optimus Prime, "especially for organic life forms."

Someone watches them from a secret lab.
It's Megatron, leader of the evil Decepticons! Megatron
would do anything to destroy his enemies, the Autobots. He sees
the dinosaurs on his monitor and hatches a plan.

"Those dinosaurs will be my new army," Megatron says.
He programs the robot dinosaurs to attack the Autobots! Now the robots are alive. They are dinobots!

Megatron sends the dinobots to find Optimus and his friends. The T. rex spots the Autobots outside Dino-World.

"Cars and trucks bad! Car robots worse!" he growls. The dinobots attack!

The Autobots fight back. Prowl dodges flames from the triceratops.

Ratchet and Bumblebee trade blasts with the giant T. rex.
"Wow, those guys are strong!" says Bumblebee.

Optimus turns the flying dinobot's fiery breath into steam.

"Get it in gear, Bulkhead!" Optimus shouts.

"Got it!" Bulkhead responds. He slams into the triceratops dinobot.

"Bumblebee!" Ratchet calls. "Add your Electro-Blast to my Magnetic Field!"

"I'm on it!" Bumblebee answers.

They attack together, creating an electromagnetic pulse.

The pulse scrambles the dinobots' circuits.
It shuts the three oversized robots down!

But not for long!
The dinobots get back up. Now they are stronger than ever!
"We have to get them off the street," Bulkhead suggests.
"Good idea!" Prime agrees.

The Autobots transform into vehicle mode. They lead the dinobots off the street and into an empty parking lot.

The dinobots start breathing scorching flames at their enemies. The pavement melts.

Optimus Prime gets an idea.

"Quick, melt the tar!" he shouts.

The Autobots start firing at the ground.

With the dinobots also shooting fire, the tar gets soft.

"We need to get them in there," orders Prime.

"I'll take care of it!" offers Bulkhead.

He charges and slams the dinobots into the gooey melted tar.

Now the dinobots are stuck! They can't fight their way out of the tar.
The Autobots saved the day!

"Thank you," Mr. Sumdac says to the Autobots later. "I have the dinobots in an energy cage now. That will keep them from causing any more trouble."

"Great," Bumblebee replies. "Maybe now we can enjoy the rest of Dino-World!"

"I think I've had enough dinosaurs for now," says Bulkhead.

The other Autobots laugh.

But in his secret lab, Megatron is not amused. "I'll defeat you Autobots yet!" he vows.